This book belongs to:

. . . .

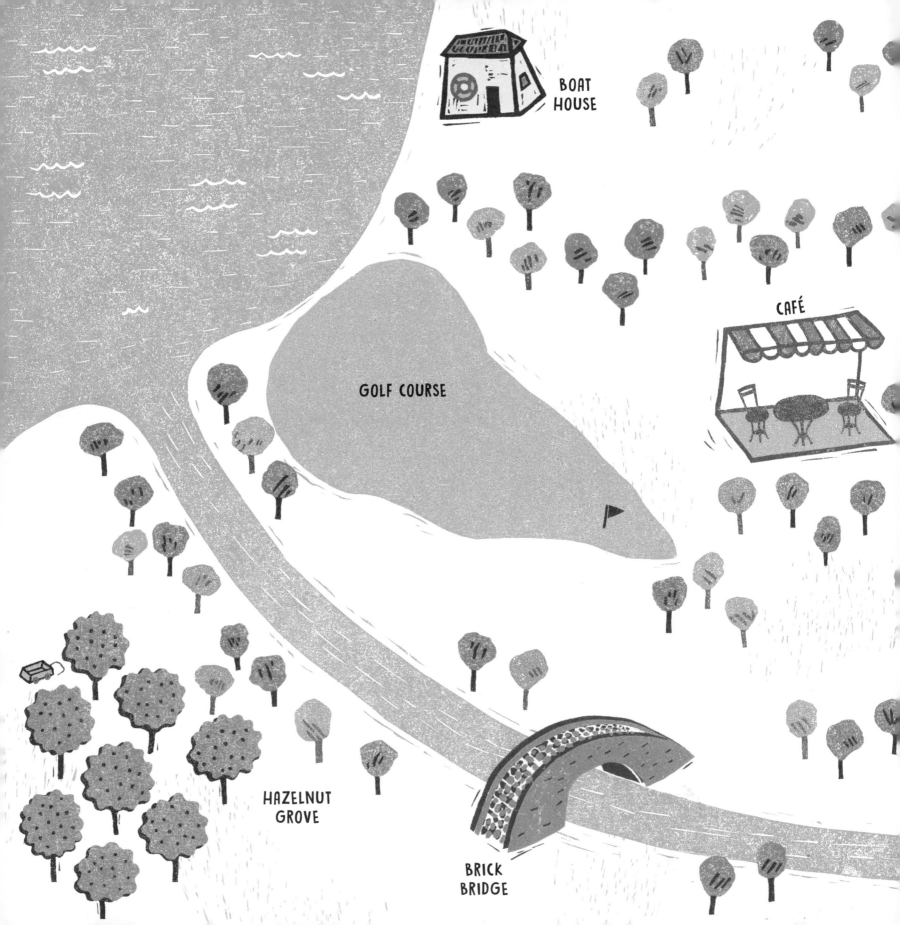

BOAT
HOUSE

CAFÉ

GOLF COURSE

HAZELNUT
GROVE

BRICK
BRIDGE

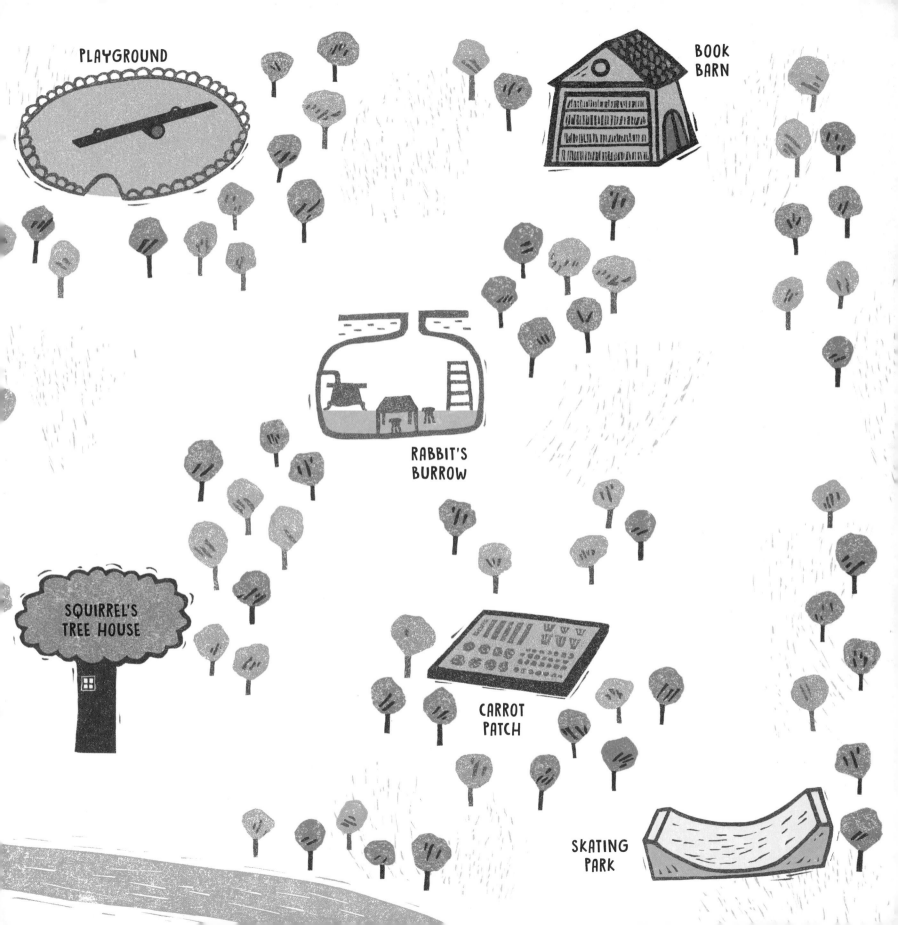

To Elsa and Georgina for helping me to follow my dream.

OXFORD
UNIVERSITY PRESS

Great Clarendon Street, Oxford, OX2 6DP,
United Kingdom

Oxford University Press is a department of the University of Oxford.
It furthers the University's objective of excellence in research,
scholarship, and education by publishing worldwide. Oxford is a
registered trade mark of Oxford University Press in the UK and in
certain other countries

Text and illustrations © Maria S. Costa 2016
The moral rights of the author have been asserted

Database right Oxford University Press (maker)

First published in 2016

British Library Cataloguing in Publication Data available

ISBN: 978-019-274627-6 (paperback)

1 3 5 7 9 10 8 6 4 2

Printed in China

Paper used in the production of this book is a natural, recyclable
product made from wood grown in sustainable forests.
The manufacturing process conforms to the environmental
regulations of the county of origin.

How to find a friend

Maria S. Costa

OXFORD
UNIVERSITY PRESS

When Squirrel moved into
her new tree house,
she thought she might meet
a friend at the playground.

But she didn't.

'Pssst!
I'll help Squirrel
find a friend!'

When Rabbit moved into
his new burrow,
he thought the café
might be a good place
to meet a friend.

But it wasn't.

'Hey!
I'll help Rabbit
find a friend!'

'Supposing I'm the only animal in the wood?' wondered Squirrel.

'But you're not!'

'What if I'm all alone
in the whole wide wood?'
pondered Rabbit.

'Look up there!'

'It's such a shame that there's nobody around,' said Rabbit.

'I've searched high
and low for a friend!'
sighed Squirrel.

THUD!

'You need
to search lower!'

'Never say never!'

'Maybe I'm never going to find a friend,' sighed Rabbit.

'At least I have
my books for company,'
said Squirrel.

'How about a rabbit for company?'

'If I keep myself busy perhaps
I won't feel so lonely,' said Rabbit.

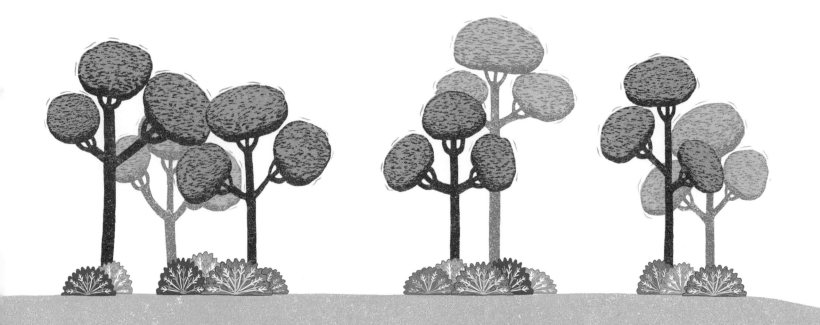

'If you keep going in this direction,
you definitely won't feel so lonely!'

'Oh my!'
said Squirrel.

SH!

'What a surprise!'
said Rabbit.

'How come I never saw
you before?' asked Squirrel.

'That's just what I was going to say!' laughed Rabbit.

'If only they'd listened to us!'

'Perhaps they don't speak Bug!'

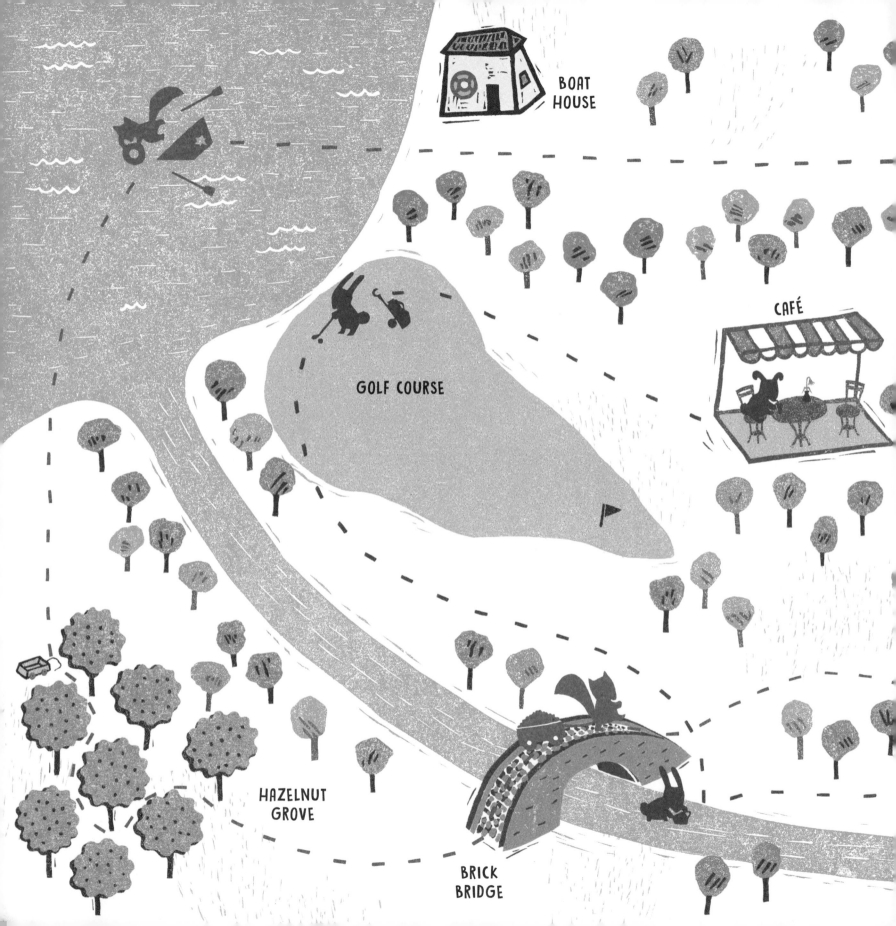

BOAT
HOUSE

CAFÉ

GOLF COURSE

HAZELNUT
GROVE

BRICK
BRIDGE

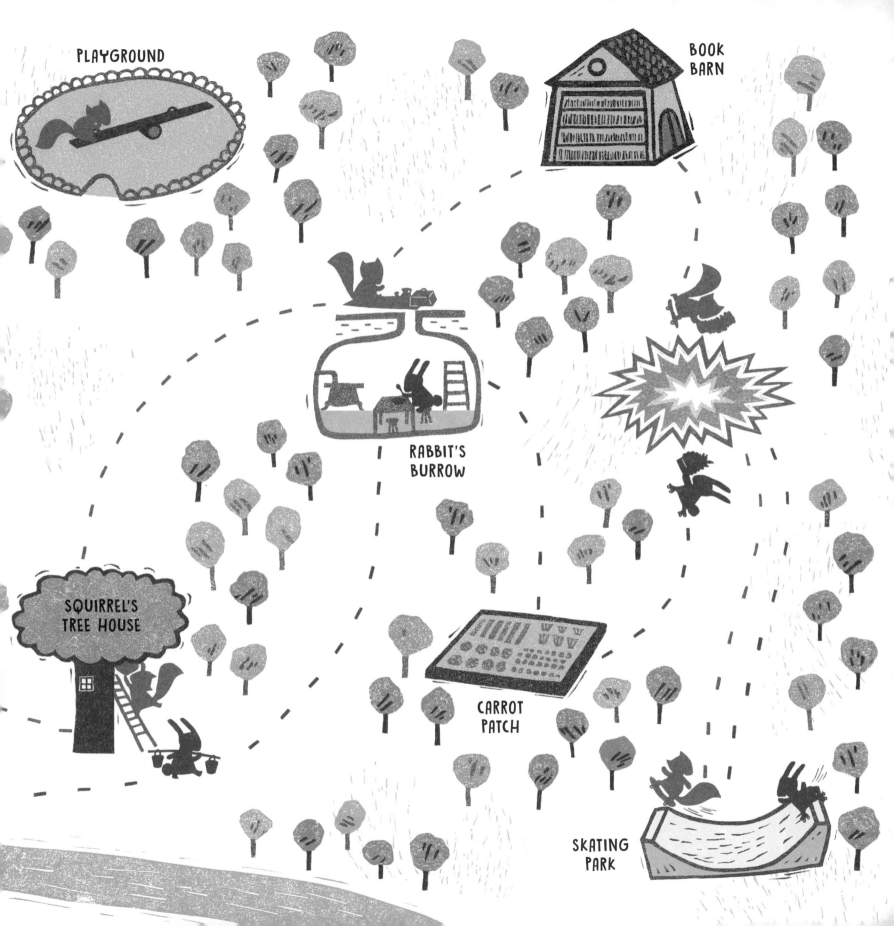

PLAYGROUND

BOOK BARN

RABBIT'S BURROW

SQUIRREL'S TREE HOUSE

CARROT PATCH

SKATING PARK

A note for grown-ups

Oxford Owl is a FREE and easy-to-use website packed with support and advice about everything to do with reading.

Informative videos

Hints, tips and fun activities

Top tips from top writers for reading with your child

Help with choosing picture books

For this expert advice and much, much more about how children learn to read and how to keep them reading ...

LOOK

for Oxford Owl

www.oxfordowl.co.uk